Unholy Night

M VIOLET

A Note from the Author

Unholy Night is a why choose dark romance novella intended for 18+ readers only. This book is dark and depraved and is not suitable for everyone.

If you are looking for a warm fuzzy holiday romance, you've picked up the wrong book. There are no heroes in this story, only villains. The FMC is selfish and snarky, and the four MMCs are completely unhinged and irredeemable. The smut is the plot. If that all sounds like your cup of tea, then keep reading, and buckle up for a quick and wild ride.

Trigger Warnings
Graphic language
Graphic sex
Graphic violence
Assault
Praise
Degradation
Non-Con
Dub-Con
BDSM
Group sex
MF, MFMMM
Choking
Spitting
Breath play
Food play
Anal
Spanking

To all my dark romance besties who like their cocoa spiked, their holidays smutty, and their book boyfriends feral AF.

Unholy Night

Chapter 1

EASTON

please fasten your seatbelts and prepare for takeoff.

No way out now.

I downed the rest of my champagne before handing it to the flight attendant. Fuck me.

"Excuse me, aren't you Easton Radleigh?"

Ugh. Fuck me twice.

I turned toward seat A11, the biggest smile plastered on my face. "Only sometimes."

The mousey-haired woman with more bubble than my champagne beamed back at me. "Oh! I just love your books. I'm a huge fan. I can't believe I'm sitting next to you. Can you believe my luck?"

I did my best not to vomit a little in my mouth. It wasn't her. It was me. I was a joke. A sham. How could I possibly be a best-selling romance author when I couldn't even write my own happy ending? I was five hours fresh off the worst breakup in history. A category five level dumping.

I smiled sweetly. "Thank you so much. You're too kind."

She was un fucking fazed. "I'm Betty by the way. Ahhh! My friend Doreen is never going to believe it. We just finished your latest, *Forbidden Viking*, for book club. We dressed up in costume and *even drank a mead*." She looked around as if the mere mention of alcohol was scandalous.

I winced as the flight attendant handed me my scotch. "Amazing. I hope you all enjoyed it." Little did Betty know, I wrote that book in between vibrators while binge watching *The Last Kingdom* after breakup number two this year.

Betty held up her glass of iced tea. *"Enjoyed it?* We loved it. Skol!" She giggled.

I clanked my glass to hers, suddenly envious of how hopeful she was. Betty probably had a decent marriage. Maybe not perfect but I'm guessing her Friday night didn't require batteries.

"Yeah, *Skol*," I muttered back.

Betty took a big gulp of her iced tea and shook her head. "Easton Radleigh. Wow."

Wowee.

"That's me." Romance author. Morbidly single. Couldn't even keep a plant alive. Even nature was trying to get away from me.

I listened to Betty talk about book club for the rest of the flight. I had three more scotches and took way too many selfies with her. I even committed to making an appearance at her next book club. At the end of the day, fans like her were the reason I kept writing.

If I could fool the world into thinking love existed, maybe I could fool myself too.

"Alright, Betty. Now you have my assistant's phone number and email. We'll set something up after the holidays."

Betty threw her arms around me, almost knocking me over. "It was fate, Miss Radleigh. I just knew things were looking up for me."

I was never good with touchy feely stuff, so I awkwardly patted her on the back mid-hug. "I'm honored, but I'm sure you have way more exciting things to celebrate than meeting little old me."

Suddenly her face fell. "I-um, don't want to be a downer, but... my husband left me recently. For a younger woman. *After thirty-five years.* I was devastated. But your books got me through it. They... well, they showed me that I can still have adventure and spice. That my person might still be out there."

Fuck me three times.

Shit.

Did I mention that I have a horrible habit of prejudging people? Yeah, I'm a real fucking piece of work. Not vain or spoiled, just bitter and cynical about literally everything.

I squeezed her shoulders. "Betty, listen to me. Fuck that asshole."

Her eyes widened.

"No, for real. You don't need him or his limp dick. His new young girlfriend is going to be faking orgasms until the day he dies. That's not on you. You tell those girls at book club that I will be seeing you all real soon."

I almost lost her until that last part. She hugged me again. "Easton Radleigh. Wow."

As I wrestled my suitcase off the baggage carousel, I swear I heard her yell *skol* a few more times.

And this is how I dealt with breakup number three—in the back of an Uber with a flask of whiskey I bought at the gift shop as I headed to a cute bed and breakfast by myself on Christmas Eve. I think I've reached a new low.

"You're lucky you made your flight, miss. This storm is about to sweep away half the eastern hemisphere. I bet your family is gonna be really happy to see ya."

Oh, a chatty driver. Great.

"What's our ETA?" Family? What are we besties?

He narrowed his eyes at me in the mirror and cleared his throat. "Right. Well, there's a lot of ice on the road so I gotta drive slowly. Should have you at the Briar Patch in about an hour."

I sighed and leaned my head back against the leather seats. All I wanted was a hot shower, more whiskey, and a good night's sleep. The cute old lady, whose picture was on the website, assured me I would have all of those things for the weekend.

The sleep part would be the challenge. Ever since Jake left me, I hadn't been able to close my eyes for more than a few hours. It wasn't that I was particularly heartbroken. He chewed with his mouth open and was rude to restaurant servers.

No. He wasn't the one. I knew that. It was the rejection. The tale as old as time of Easton Radleigh getting less action than the characters in her books. The sad fact that I could write beautiful love stories while my own love life was a fucking disaster.

I took another swig from my flask as the Uber driver eyed me. "It's juice."

"It's noon," he muttered under his breath.

Fuck. Just let me have my juice. It's not like *I'm* driving for fuck's sake. "I know what time it is, thank you."

We drove in silence the rest of the way. I pressed my face to the window, the cool glass felt amazing on my cheeks, *I was kind of drunk,* and gazed out at the abomination of nature. It's not that I hated the outdoors. The outdoors hated me. It was beautiful though. Still and peaceful and untainted by society. That's why I chose this place. It was just far enough in the middle of nowhere that I wouldn't be tempted to do anything stupid. *Like crawl into bed with some wall street executive with martini breath and a pinky ring.*

The snow fell harder as we pulled into what looked like a town. There were a few streetlights flickering, rusty tin signs flapping in the wind, and a few buildings that looked like they were abandoned in the ice age.

The car slowed to a stop in front of the only building with a light still on. Oh, did I say light? Let me rephrase. LIGHTS. Like a million of them. All red and green and strung around every inch of the place like it was being suffocated by Saint Nick himself.

Fuck me four times.

"Um, where the hell are we?"

The driver rolled his eyes. I *saw* his fucking eyes roll at me in the mirror. "Your destination. The Briar Patch Inn."

The pictures online showed it to be more of a Gothic baroque style Victorian with charm and pizazz. A place I pictured sipping mimosas at on their French patio. No. This was the makings of a rest home for crazy cat ladies. Fuck. Now that I thought about it. That little old lady in the picture did have a cat on her lap.

5

The driver sprinted up to the front entrance with my luggage before I was even on the sidewalk. He must be a plant. Fuck him.

"Merry Christmas," he muttered.

"Yup. Thanks." Ugh. Whatever. I was not a monster. Not totally. I clicked on the app and left him an extra tip. The least I could do for making him deal with my bullshit. I couldn't help it. I had zero filter.

I traipsed up the steps and almost fell twice, cursing at myself for wearing heels and not proper winter shoes. I still believed that people should dress up when they got on an airplane. Besides, I had no idea what proper winter shoes were. I mean Southern California gets its windstorms but we're hardly walking around in snowshoes.

I pushed open the door to the inn and nearly fainted. My stomach clenched as I took in the sight. Well, as much as I could before I was almost blinded by all the twinkling lights. It was like someone had stuffed Christmas into a pinata and then broke it open violently.

I'm going to be sick.

"You lost, beautiful?" His voice was raspy like cigars and whiskey.

I turned toward the front desk to see a man. No. Like a fucking man. With the body of a god, if gods wore tight black T-shirts and jeans, had dark brown hair in an actual man bun, and green eyes that were somehow more piercing than the fucking Christmas lights that were making my stigmatism flare up.

He was behind the desk. Like he worked here. No, no, no.

"Unfortunately not. I'm checking in."

The man smoothed his hands over his abs, which appeared to not have a single ounce of body fat on them, and smirked. "Sure. Come on over."

I stalked over to the desk and slammed my purse down. "Where's the cute old lady from the photo? Where are the cats? I mean, *you* don't even have a name tag."

The man cocked his head to the side and did this thing with his lip that was somewhere between a pout and a snarl. Fuck. I need to stop staring at his lips. His soft, thick lips. No. Stop it!

He clicked his pen. "Oh, you mean my grandmother. Sweet thing. Yeah she died. Me and my partners run the inn now. Sorry, I forgot my name tag in the back. My name's Roman."

A shiver ran through me. "Partners? This isn't the Hyatt. How many assholes does it take to run a twelve-room bed and breakfast?"

Roman leaned forward on his elbows, grinning as if I was the most amusing thing he'd seen all day. "Well, there's check in, cooking, cleaning… you'd be surprised how dirty it can get around here."

By the way he winked, I was sure that he was used to that being a surefire panty-dropper, but it only pissed me off more. "Okay, Casanova, let's get one thing straight. I have three days to finish my book. Three fucking days. Now as long as you keep the food coming, the power on, and the other guests in check, we'll get along just fine, and I'll leave you an amazing Yelp review."

"Credit card and ID please, darlin'," Roman drawled, totally ignoring everything I said in typical male fashion.

His eyes only slightly deviated from the computer screen when I took a huge pull from my flask. But it was subtle. This guy was good. He didn't miss a beat. But there was no way this hot lumber jack was running Santa's toy shop-slash-inn. Aside from the twenty-seven variations of Santa dolls lining the floor, there were three

Christmas trees in this room for fuck's sake. *Three.* Really? It was creepy as fuck.

Roman, AKA, hot ruler of Santa Land, placed a key card on the counter. "Alright, Miss Radleigh. You're in the North Pole room. I'll have Penn grab your bags and show you up."

What the actual fuck?

"Excuse me, North Pole room? Your inn doesn't use fucking numbers?" My armpits were sweating now. Yup. I could smell my deodorant working overtime.

Roman held onto his charm like a fucking leprechaun. "Yes, ma'am. Christmas was my grandmother's favorite holiday. May she rest in peace."

Oh, I've done it now. I was going to be in one of those Netflix docuseries. I could see it now: romance author unlucky in love, checks into Christmas horror house and gets chopped up into little pieces by hot lumberjacks.

"Right. Whatever." I took another swig. "Where's Pencil?"

"It's Penn." Another one. Ripped in a tight T-shirt. Blond wavy hair. Blue eyes. Looks like he walks around with an airbrush filter. Fuck.

I was a bit drunk but even a sober person would think this was all a bit much. "Sorry, *Penn.*"

He made sure to flex his muscles as he picked up my luggage. He snickered as I followed him up the very old and very creaky stairs. "You sure you're just here for the weekend? This bag weighs more than my car."

Oh, a cheeky one. Awesome. "If it's too heavy for you, *pencil,* I'm sure I can manage."

He stopped abruptly, causing me to bump into his back. As he turned around, my heart raced. My mouth always got me in trouble. Shit. They could be like sweet hot lumber jack innkeepers by day and serial killers by night.

Penn's lips curled up into a smirk. "You're fucking feisty. And I'm here for it."

I rolled my eyes but inside my belly was fluttering. There was something about the way he was looking at me. Like I was a meal to be devoured. It made me uneasy. But I wasn't sure yet if that was a good or bad thing.

By the time we reached the North Pole—never thought I'd use that in a sentence—my blond lumberjack was now ogling every inch of my body. Another reason why I should have worn ugly snowshoes instead of heels.

I handed him a twenty-dollar bill. "Thank you, *Penn.*"

He looked at me like I had three heads. "I'm not taking your money."

"It's a tip. For carrying my luggage." Holy Christmas balls what was wrong with this place?

He stepped into me, a little too close. "Where I come from, we don't charge women for carrying their bags. It's called being a gentleman."

Maybe it was the six-hour flight or the copious amounts of whiskey I've consumed, but something about the way Penn was standing, the way he drawled that all out, turned me on more than I cared to admit.

"Great line. I'm gonna use that one." I gave him a wink before I closed the door.

Chapter 2

ROMAN

"I told you to lock the fucking front door, Penn."

The night was almost over. Almost. Until that bombshell walked in. We were just hours away from getting what we wanted.

Penn threw up his hands. "Are you fucking kidding me? You said you cancelled all the reservations."

Fuck. I never mess up. Ever. "I thought I did. It must have slipped through the cracks."

"Yeah *and* you checked her in. Could have turned her away but you took one look at her big tits and tight ass and your brain fell into your dick."

"Like you weren't fucking ogling her on the stairs. Fuck off. What was I supposed to do? Throw her out into the storm?"

Penn ran a hand through his blond hair. "Roman, *the basement*. She knows what we look like."

"I know. Fuck. Just let me think."

"This motherfucker won't talk." Zander waltzed into the room, wiping blood off his knife with a kitchen towel. He took one look at us and paused. "What's going on? Why do you two assholes look like you just shit yourselves?"

His black hair was matted to his forehead. That was the thing about Zander, it didn't matter if he was sweating, bleeding, or coming, his hair never fucking moved. And yes, I've seen him do all three.

"We have a situation," I muttered.

"You know I hate that word, Roman," Vance spat as he joined the party.

Fuck him. "Situation?"

He snickered. "*We*. If there's a situation, it's all you. The rest of us did our fucking part."

Penn shook his head as he scrolled through his phone. "Oh, it gets fucking worse. She's famous. Like really fucking famous."

My stomach sank. No fucking way. "I've never seen or heard of her before."

"That's because you don't read romance novels, Rom," Penn spat.

Zander crossed his arms. "What in the ever-loving fuck is going on?"

This was fucking bad. How the hell were we supposed to carry out the job without witnesses when we had one fucking witness upstairs in the North Pole? And who the fuck uses Christmas related names instead of room numbers? This place was already giving me the creeps and now I had to deal with some mouthy, although, extremely hot woman snapping her fingers at us like we're her pool boys.

"There's a guest upstairs. One of the reservations didn't get cancelled… It's gonna be fine. If she's really that famous author, she'll probably be holed up in her room the whole time writing or something." I moved to the door and locked all three deadbolts. "Once we get the info we need, we're out."

Vance leaned across the front desk and sniffed the air like a fucking bloodhound. "Chanel. Expensive. High maintenance." He shook his head, sliding a hand through his light brown hair. "Nah, she ain't holing up in her room all weekend. Great job, Roman. Now we have two fucking hostages."

I looked around, speechless. He was right. Fuck. In the ten years we'd been pulling jobs together, this was my first big fuck up. Usually that honor went to Penn. I was the one who was always three steps ahead of everyone else. The four of us were professionals but sometimes shit got dicey and a slip up would happen. Just never because of me.

Penn was right. I took one look at her dark brown hair, green eyes, and banging body, and I checked out while my cock checked her in. Fucking literally.

Zander smirked, amused by the beating I was internally giving myself. He knew me better than anyone and could read me like a fucking book. "I only see a couple ways out of this, boys… Either we kill Mr. Basement, pretend we actually run this place, and then wish Miss Famous Romance Author well when she checks out on

Monday. *Or* we kill them both right now and get the fuck out of here."

Vance nodded. "I vote for door number two. If I have to spend three nights in the fifth ring of Christmas hell, I'm going to off myself."

Penn fingered one of the many brightly colored lights framing the door. "Except you didn't see her... Rom and I did. She was fucking sexy as hell. Isn't that right, Rom?"

My cock stirred in my pants. Again. I nodded. "She also talked more shit than my Uncle Tony. Not some dumb chick any of us can manipulate."

Zander perked up. "Is that a challenge?"

Vance chuckled. "You've gone and done it now, Rom."

"We have a job to finish," I snapped. "Let's just get through this weekend and then we never have to see her or the basement asshole ever again. I mean, how hard can it be to look after one hotel guest?"

I had seen some really fucked up shit in my life—sickness, torture, dead crazy cat ladies in meat lockers—but the thought of waiting on some famous rich girl for three days was actually making me nauseous. But what choice did we have? I didn't kill women. *We* didn't kill women. Zander was just trying to rile me up even more.

Penn spit in his hand and held it out. "Then it's settled. We make that piece of shit talk, take care of Miss Radleigh for the weekend, and then we're out."

Vance threw his head back and laughed as he spit in his hand and slapped Penn's. "I'm in just to watch Penny boy here grovel for some rich bitch pussy."

13

Zander's eyes darkened as he too spit and shook Penn's hand. "Maybe we all will. Wouldn't be the first time…"

As much shit as we spewed at each other, we were closer than brothers. Tighter than Robin's band of merry thieves. We've shared a lot of things over the years. *Women included.*

I was the last to solidify the pact with a hard grip on Penn's hand. "Let's try to keep our dicks in our pants this time."

I looked around at my partners, noticing how they each had that mischievous glimmer in their eyes. I had a sinking feeling that this weekend might not go as planned. But I always was the pessimist of the group. Now we all just had to get our stories straight so little miss feisty didn't figure out what we were really doing here.

Chapter 3

EASTON

"*He kissed her with a passion he didn't know he had…*" My fingers stilled on the keyboard.

"And then what?" *Fuck.* Writing this book was like pulling teeth.

I slammed my laptop shut and looked out the window. Well, I tried to look out the window through the blinding web of Christmas lights draped across it.

This room was offensive. The bed was covered with pillows shaped and decorated like Christmas presents. There was a tree in the corner that had so many ornaments on it, I wondered how it was still standing upright. Even the carpet was white and sparkly. *I'm guessing to look like snow?* That will teach me to book something on the internet without checking the reviews.

There was no television, no complimentary bottled water, no fancy amenities in the bathroom—unless you count the reindeer soaps and the elf toothbrush holder—and no room service. Ugh. *Why me?*

My stomach grumbled. The only thing I managed to get down on the flight was scotch and an over-salted bag of peanuts.

I needed a shower and a good night's sleep even though I knew it was too early to go to bed. This fucking time difference was killing me. But I needed food more than insomnia right now.

I sighed as I changed into a pair of jeans and my favorite black cashmere sweater. I tossed my brown hair up into a bun and threw on some silver hoops. As I laced up my black leather boots, I wondered if those hot lumberjacks were capable of whipping up a decent meal.

The website claimed that dinner was included with the room. I figured I'd still go into town to a nice restaurant but there didn't seem to be any. I glanced out the window again, looking for any signs of life. "Fucking miserable small-town bullshit," I mumbled. This Christmas massacre of an inn really was the only place open.

It's okay, you can do this, Easton. Just march out there and demand a hot meal. I creaked the door open halfway and peered down the hall. It was too quiet for this time of night. The other guests must already be downstairs.

Halfway down the stairs, without warning, the song *Jingle Bells* blasted out of the speakers. I ducked as if somehow the sound of it might knock me out. "What the fuck?" I crouched against the banister, a bit over dramatic I know, but holy hell it was loud. Oh, and did I mention I *hate* Christmas. Like loathe it.

A barrage of male voices, cursing and yelling, carried over from another room. "Turn that shit off!" one of them yelled. "It's fucking stuck. Hold on," another one fired back.

My head pounded as the creepy chorus of children's voices seemed to grow louder. I envisioned psycho little Christmas dolls with those open and shut eyes. Yeah, I hated dolls too. Fuck, I really was a piece of work. My last therapist made me sit in a room full of them to *face my fears*. I fired that bitch so fast.

Like a vacuum sucking all the sanity out of my head, the music finally stopped. I rubbed my ringing ears. "Fucking finally."

"You think you're gonna live?" a low voice snickered.

I looked up to see a man. *Another one?* I gazed up the length of his hard body, tight abs stretching out his black T-shirt, broad shoulders, tattoos covering his arms and neck, black hair, and brown eyes. Sexy as hell with a shit grin on his face. Fuck.

Realizing I probably looked like a complete idiot sitting on the stairs, gripping the banister for dear life, I popped up with a little too much pep and stumbled forward. The man caught me on the last step.

He sniffed the air between us. "Are you drunk?"

I pushed against his chest and took a giant leap back. Yep, definitely perfect solid muscle. "More like deaf now thanks to the surround sound. I think my ears are bleeding."

He leaned his massive frame against the banister, and I was actually concerned that he might break it. "Rom said you had a mouth on you. He just didn't tell me how sexy it was."

I rolled my eyes, fighting the flush that was creeping across my cheeks. "Great. You work here too. Just great."

His eyes lingered a little too long on my hips. "Easton Radleigh." He stuck out his hand. "I'm Zander."

Ignoring his hand, I brushed past him into the dining room. There were three long tables set for six and a couple of tables for two. The plates and tablecloths were of course made to look like they came straight from Santa's workshop. It was a sea of red and green glitter.

"Where are all the other guests?" It was 5 PM and the place was empty. Plus, I thought it was odd that not a single person had come out to yell about the music.

A door swung open and in waltzed more man candy. He was tall, slender but just as ripped as Zander, with brown hair and light green eyes. Fucking gorgeous. What was this? A hot lumberjack convention?

"What other guests?" The new one snickered.

My stomach dropped. "The *other guests* that are staying here."

"It's just you, baby." He winked and plopped down into a tinsel-wrapped chair.

No, no, no. This can't be happening. "Okay, first of all, don't call me *baby*. Second, that's impossible. When I booked, I had to settle for a regular room because all the suites were sold out. And third, instead of sitting on your ass, maybe you could, oh, I don't know, get me a drink or something. You know if it's not too inconvenient for you."

Something wild flickered in his eyes. He stood and walked into me, forcing me back against the wall. Towering over me, he placed both hands on the wall, boxing me in. "First of all," he began, mimicking me, "the inn *was* fully booked but everyone checked out before the storm." He pressed his chest against mine. "Second, I will happily get you a drink if you ask nicely." His lips hovered over my ear, his breath tickling me. "And third… I think you liked it when I called you baby."

Holy fuck, I couldn't breathe. This man was fucking hot.

"Let her go, Vance."

I blinked and finally forced myself to look away from Vance's striking green eyes. Roman and Penn were here too now. Four of the sexiest men I'd ever seen and me, just me, trapped in the inn that murdered Christmas. For three nights. Shit.

Vance chuckled and backed off, returning to his tinsel-covered chair.

"Sorry about that, Miss Radleigh. Vance is harmless. Just an asshole," Roman quipped as he shot the man in question a dirty look.

There was no way in reindeer hell that any of these fuckboy-looking specimens were harmless. Not a chance. They might as well have been wearing T-shirts that said, *I'll give you the best fuck of your life and then you'll never hear from me again.*

I waved him off, annoyed, and strutted to the farthest table in the room—one by the window that was set for two. "Can I get a menu, please, or do you all have an *Only Fans* meeting you need to get to?"

Snickers and chuckles erupted from the snarky little group of man junk. The testosterone was so thick in this room you could practically cut it and slice it.

Roman, the one who checked me in, laid a blank piece of paper in front of me.

I sighed extra loud. "What, you want an autograph first?"

He clicked his pen and offered it to me. "Write down what you want to eat, and we'll do our best to make it."

Oh, for fuck's sake. I snatched the pen out of his hand. "Anything? Like if I write down champagne and caviar, you're just going to go back there, wave your magic Christmas wand, and poof, there it is?" I highly doubted there were tins of caviar floating around this monstrosity. Champagne maybe.

Vance snorted. "That's what you want for dinner? Caviar? Not very filling."

Oh my god. These assholes were stepping on my last nerve. "*I know that* and no I don't want caviar for dinner. I'm just trying to make a point." I waved the pen in his direction. "You want me to write down what I want but I don't even know what you have."

Zander approached the table and knelt down. *So patronizing.* "How about this, beautiful, you let us come up with something tasty for you. Any allergies we should know about?"

I looked around, all four of them grinning like they were up to no good and sank back against my chair. "Fine. But I swear to God if you bring me a fucking gingerbread house, I'm going to lose it. And *please* someone pour me a drink." I glared at Zander.

Roman chuckled. "Vance go get Miss Radleigh a drink."

"Sorry, but I don't know how to make a cosmopolitan," he snickered.

Ugh, douchebag. "What, your mom never taught you how she likes them? I'll take a whiskey straight thanks. Make it a double. You know what, fuck it. Just bring me a glass and the bottle."

Penn burst out laughing. "I like her."

"Fuck off, *Pencil*," Vance snapped as he walked back into what I assumed was the kitchen.

Roman and Penn followed behind, but Zander lingered for a moment; his gaze fixated on mine. "What's a woman like you doing in the middle of nowhere on Christmas Eve?"

A knot formed in my stomach. "A woman like what exactly?"

He licked his lips. His full sexy mouth-watering lips. "Smart, rich, stunning as hell… I would think a woman like you would have a boyfriend, a husband, or at least a friend with benefits to spend the holidays with."

I sucked in a sharp breath. Everyone always assumed my life was perfect. That the famous Easton Radleigh always got her way. "Who says I don't?" I snapped.

Zander leaned in closer, his muscled arm gripping the back of my chair. "Bullshit… some asshole broke your heart. That's what you're running away from, isn't it?"

I could feel my cheeks flame as I scooted away from him. "Oh, you think you have me all figured out, don't you? Why I'm here is none of your business. Why are you fucking here?"

At that he tensed and backed up. "I'm just a humble innkeeper."

It was my turn to laugh. I looked him up and down. "Right. How about you go check on my drink then? I hope he didn't have to go to Scotland to get it." I was being extra bitchy, but my stomach was grumbling, my head pounded with a splitting headache, and I hadn't been fucked properly in three months.

Zander's lip twitched, a feral look glazing his eyes as he looked at me. "One of these days someone is going to make you shut that feisty mouth of yours," he rasped.

Fuck. Sweat beaded between my thighs. At least I hoped it was sweat. I was playing with fire now. But I just couldn't stop myself. I stood up and walked into his space. "Yeah? And do you think that's going to be you, big man? You going to shut me up?" My heart was racing.

He looked down at me and smiled. "Well, it'll be kind of hard to talk with my cock in—"

"Whoa!" Roman yelled. "Zander, bro, chill."

Vance snickered as he set a glass and a bottle of whiskey down on my table. "I always miss the good shit."

My breath hitched as I glared at Zander, refusing to back down or give in. "I'm going to give you the worst review on Yelp."

He smirked and backed away. "Sure, sure. Whatever you say. I'm just messing around."

"Let's all give Miss Radleigh some space, guys." He poured me some whiskey from the bottle. "You'll have to excuse my partners; they haven't been around a classy woman like yourself for some time."

As they left the room, I rolled my eyes at their backs. But despite his raunchiness, I was strangely turned on by Zander. By all of them actually. *Ugh. Well, that can't be good.* I couldn't really have all four of them.

I could see the headline now: *Esteemed romance author, Easton Radleigh turns into a massive slut over the weekend. Christmas came and so did she.*

Fuck, the sad part was it would actually be less embarrassing than the story the papers have currently been running about me.

They just love reminding me of how I got dumped for the third time this year.

I swallowed down two shots of whiskey in a matter of minutes as I gazed out the frosted window. There was nothing but darkness as far as the eye could see. The paparazzi would never find me here. It was the only silver lining in this disaster of a trip.

Chapter 4

ZANDER

What a fucking mouth that one had on her. Fuck. *The balls.* If she only knew who the fuck we really were, she'd be pissing in her pants. I meant what I said. Easton Radleigh would be much better off with my cock in her mouth. Fuck. I was rock hard just thinking about it.

"Quit pouting, Z. She's just a spoiled brat who's used to people waiting on her without blinking." Roman motioned for me to keep chopping.

I had zoned out over a half-diced onion, completely dumbstruck over that beautiful headcase in the dining room. "What are we even doing, Rom? We're not fucking innkeepers, or cooks for that matter. I don't think I can deal with her attitude all weekend."

Vance propped himself up on the center island, not lifting a finger as usual. "Z's right. We're *on a fucking job*, Rom. There's a man tied up in the basement. And you got us running around here like we're on some HGTV show. I say we throw her down there with that asshole downstairs."

Penn wiped the sweat off his brow with his free arm as he stirred a big pot of tomato sauce. "Fuck that, Vance. You know we don't hurt women. Not gonna happen."

Vance's eyes lit up. "Hurt her? Nah, I'm talking about making her cum so fucking hard she'll be saying please and thank you by morning. Guaranteed she looks hot as hell in handcuffs."

He had a point. "That chick is a monster. Maybe getting tied up and gagged would teach her some fucking manners." Fuck, she was really getting under my skin.

"I bet she'd like it too. All that pent up aggression… *fuck*," Penn rasped as he readjusted his cock.

Rom gripped the edge of the counter. "Enough. Easton Radleigh is as cold as ice. There's no point in even fucking talking about it. Just stick to the plan and we'll all be sipping margaritas in Cabo by Monday."

We all nodded in agreement while continuing to make Easton a halfway decent bowl of pasta. When you live life on the run, never stopping too long in one place, you became really good at eating out. None of us had ever cooked for ourselves, let alone a woman. But Rom and Penn had watched enough food shows to have an idea.

After dicing up an onion and two cloves of garlic, I handed Penn the cutting board for him to dump it all in the sauce. A bottle of red wine caught my eye in the pantry. That was one thing I did know for sure, red wine and marinara sauce paired well together.

Fuck knows I've had my share of both. I opened the bottle and poured each of us a glass.

Vance smirked. "Remember that time we drank three bottles of wine and ate an entire six-course Italian dinner with that fucker strung up in the warehouse?"

I nodded, laughing uncontrollably now. "Fucker kept moaning every time I took a bite of my meatball."

Rom snorted. "He screamed louder watching you eat than he did when Vance hit him."

"I'm still convinced that's the only reason why he talked. Fuck the blood coming out of his eyes, that asshole was starving," Penn chimed in.

"Oh, shit that's funny." My stomach hurt from laughing. These were my boys. My ride or die partners in crime. And fuck, did we know how to have a good time. This business here was just a minor setback.

I clapped Roman on the back. "You're right, man. I think we can handle one stuck-up celebrity for a few days."

He nodded. "There you go. That's what I like to hear. Now help me strain these noodles so we can feed her before she throws a fucking temper tantrum."

I carried the bowl of pasta for Easton while Rom, Vance, and Penn followed with a chunk of parmesan cheese, bread, and a bottle of red wine.

And we almost dropped all of it when we entered the dining room. Her brown hair was out of its bun, messy and loose around her shoulders and down her back. With her legs propped up on the table like it was a footstool, a billow of smoke floated above her head.

My stomach sank. She was smoking my fucking cigar. The ones we were saving for when we finish this nightmare job. I must have left it on the windowsill earlier. Without thinking, I charged over, knocked her legs off the table, and yanked the exquisitely rolled Cuban out of her mouth. "Who the fuck do you think you are?"

She flinched slightly but recovered quickly, throwing me a sloppy smile. "The brochure said for me to make myself at home."

Fuck. I started forward again but Roman grabbed my arm. "Hey, relax. Miss Radleigh is right. She's our VIP guest. Let's not forget that."

I clenched my fists at my sides imagining all the ways I wanted to punish her spoiled little cunt.

Penn pried the bowl of pasta out of my hands and set it down in front of her. "Here you go. Cheese?"

Easton batted her eyelashes at me like a fucking brat. "No, I don't do dairy."

I snatched the block of cheese off the table. "Just dairy or are you allergic to all forms of calcium?"

Vance snorted. "Damn, Z, you really wanted that cigar."

She rolled her eyes and took a big bite of pasta. "Are you all going to stand there and watch me eat?"

"Come on, guys, let's leave Miss Radleigh to her meal," Roman quickly replied before it got any more fucking awkward than it already was.

As I backed up slowly, refusing to take my eyes off her, I caught a glimpse of her crossing her legs. I bet this ice-queen hasn't been fucked properly in her entire privileged life. She wouldn't know what to do with the four of us if she tried. That thought made me so fucking hard, it took all three of my boys to guide me back to the kitchen.

But I couldn't resist.

I dashed back to the table and leaned over her from behind, my arms boxing her in. I felt her body shudder against me mid-chew. "If you clench your legs together any tighter," I whispered, "you're going to rub your pussy raw."

Her throat bobbed as she swallowed her food down hard. "How fucking dare you," she rasped back.

I breathed heavily into her ear. "Come find me if you want help... *alleviating* that later."

Chapter 5

EASTON

Between the whiskey, wine, and Zander's buttery voice, I could barely eat. I hated that he was right. I was so turned on by his whole *bad boy with a chip on his shoulder* act, I could hardly walk back to my room without clenching. But I did. I walked all the way up those nausea inducing, candy cane-lined stairs without a glance back.

I changed into a pair of black yoga pants and a matching tank top before plopping down on the bed with my laptop. I needed to try and write at least one more chapter tonight. But all I could think about was his breath in my ear. His hot, wine-soaked breath and the dirty words that unfurled from his lips.

A knock on the door made me jump and almost sent my laptop crashing to the floor.

Fuck.

"Seriously?" I called out as I charged to the door and yanked it open.

Zander stood in front of me with the half-eaten bowl of pasta I'd left on the table. "You didn't finish."

Fucking smart ass. "Yeah, I'm good. Thanks." I tried to close the door, but he wedged his foot in the crack, forcing it open. "Excuse me?"

As he stepped inside my room, he kicked the door shut behind him. "I don't know what kinds of schmucks you're used to dealing with, but I ain't the one, sweetheart. We made this for you, and you're going to fucking eat all of it."

Unfuckingbelievable. The audacity. I folded my arms and took a step back. "Get out of my room before I call security."

"What security? This is a bed and breakfast not the fucking Ritz. None of your little minions are coming to save you, princess. It's just you and us here," he snickered.

My heart raced. "What's going on here? Are you really even innkeepers?"

Zander kept walking toward me, forcing me back until the back of my legs hit the desk chair and I plopped down. He scooped a heap of pasta onto the spoon and held it in front of my mouth. "Eat. Don't make me tell you again."

Fuck. They really were going to chop me up into little pieces. *I'm so fucking fucked.* There's no cell service, no one to hear me scream… no way out. I glared at him before opening my mouth. "I will fucking sue the shit out of—"

Zander shoved the spoon into my mouth. "See, I told you I would shut you up. Now chew and swallow like a good girl."

The pasta was fucking delicious, I was just being spiteful because *they* made it. And now he was fucking feeding me while my own juices dripped down my thighs. I was practically panting like a cat in heat.

He fed me three more bites before setting the bowl down on the desk. "Why are you wound so fucking tight?"

How much time do you have? Is what I wanted to say. "So, typically when strange men break into my room and force feed me pasta, that tends to make me a little uneasy."

"You're not uneasy." He runs his thumb across my bottom lip, wiping the sauce off of it. "You've been deprived of actual fucking pleasure for so long, you don't know how to enjoy anything." He sucks the sauce off his thumb. "I bet you haven't had a good night's sleep in years, am I right?"

My heart was pounding out of my chest. He was so fucking hot. The way he stood over me, flicking his tongue across his lips. The way he looked at me like I was a trapped animal he was about to devour... It made my nipples harder than fucking icebergs.

And he was right about all of it. "You don't know me," I whispered.

He wrapped his hand around my neck. "But I want to."

I stifled a moan as he dragged his thumb down my jaw. I was frozen, completely turning to putty in his hands like one of the damsels in distress from my romance novels. Fuck. *I am not that girl.*

He slid his thumb across my lips again. "I can do things to you that will make you feel alive again... Would you like that, sweetheart? Hmm? Tell me you don't want me to ease that ache between your legs right now, and I'll walk away. Look me in the eyes and tell me."

Beads of sweat dripped down my back as the heat in my body increased. I wasn't used to men like them. Those hot, alpha men only existed in my books. Not in real life. The douchebags I'd been with were more of the wham-bam-thank-you-ma'am variety. The kind that fucked you like a jack rabbit until they came and then left you there panting in your own unfulfilled juices.

But this one... If I truly was in Christmas hell, than Zander was in charge of the devil's toy shop. And he wanted to play with every inch of me.

He smiled as if he knew he had me. "Not so sassy, now, are you?"

A spasm shot through my core. Maybe this was exactly what I needed. I could file this under romance book research, right?

"I don't... I shouldn't..." Fuck. My tongue felt like a lump of coal in my mouth.

In seconds, he hoisted me out of the chair and slinked behind me. I shivered at the feel of his hard cock pressing into my lower back. "What you *should* do, and what you *want* me to do are two very different things, beautiful." He dragged his fingers across my belly and lifted my shirt. "But I'm not going anywhere until you *finish*."

Fuck. *He's no longer talking about the pasta.*

He pulled my tank top up over my breasts as I leaned back against his chest. I almost cried tears of joy when he pinched my swollen nipples in between his fingers. "Thatta girl. Arch your back for me. *Fuck*..." He sucked on my neck with his soft full lips as he continued to rub his fingers back and forth, pinching and pulling at my tender flesh. "I bet I could make you cum just from this."

A whimper escaped my lips. "Please…"

He chuckled in my ear. "Don't worry, sweet thing. I have every intention of scratching that itch of yours."

Am I that obvious? Was I just walking around oozing vibes of the I-haven't-been-fucked-properly-in-years variety? This was so fucking wrong. He's a stranger. Possibly a serial killer. But the thought of him taking what he wanted from me sent a spasm so deep inside my core it made me feral.

He slid his hands down my waist, fingering the edges of my yoga pants. "Relax, princess, daddy's here now. I know you've been a nice girl all year. But now I want you to be naughty."

Oh, dear god. I gasped as his fingers dipped below my waistband. "Does that line really work on anyone?" I breathed. I didn't know how much longer I could pretend I wasn't enjoying this.

He chuckled in my ear. "Let's find out." Without warning, he slid his middle finger down my slit.

I bucked my hips back at the contact, my clit aching with need. I bit down on my lower lip to stifle a moan.

He nuzzled my neck. "Mmm, so wet. What were you saying about my lines?"

I whimpered as he edged his finger inside my pussy. "Fuck you," I rasped.

He grabbed a fistful of my hair and yanked my head to the side while he shoved a second finger inside me. "Yeah, you want to hate fuck me, Easton? Take all your bad relationships out on me?"

I couldn't breathe with the pressure from his thick fingers

stretching me open. Everything tingled and ached, like a storm that had been brewing for years and was finally about to hit. And I was afraid that once he started, I wouldn't want him to stop.

He pumped his fingers in and out slowly as I rolled my hips to the rhythm. "*Yes, fuck me...* You're such a dick, Zander."

"That's right, darlin'. Let me show you how *big* of a dick I can be." He shoved me toward the foot of the bed and bent me over in one swift motion. "Be a good girl and keep your hands where I can see them."

I placed my palms on the ruffled bedspread and practically drooled onto it as he yanked my pants and panties down.

"Look at that creamy-white ass just begging to be marked," he growled as he spread my legs apart.

Butterflies swarmed in my belly at the jingle of his buckle unlatching, the slither of his belt sliding out of its loops, the whizz of his zipper coming down. I felt the whoosh of air before the taut leather strap came down with a hard slap against my ass cheek, almost making me cum on the spot.

"Fuck," I cried out louder than I'd intended.

He gently rubbed the spot he slapped. "I knew all it would take is a good spanking to get you to be behave."

Fuck. His words sent more spasms to my already swollen clit. "You're an imbecile," I grunted out between whimpers.

Zander laughed. "Keep talking. Your filthy mouth turns me on." He pulled my hips back until I felt his hard exposed cock throb against my ass crack. "You look like a fucking whore right now, Easton. Do you want me to fuck you like one?"

My nipples pebbled and moisture leaked down my thighs.

Fuck. I squirmed on the bed, fighting with myself and him as he held me down. "I'm not a whore," I muttered. But I kind of liked the idea of being one for him.

He dug his fingers into my thighs and spread me wide open. The tip of his cock probed at my slick entrance. "You're my fucking whore, Easton." He inched in slightly and it was all I could do to keep from begging him not to stop. "And you're going to let me treat you like one."

I cried out as he shoved his thick cock all the way in. "Uhhh."

He slapped my ass cheeks hard as he ripped through me. "Fuck yeah, you're so tight. Open up for me. Stretch that cunt around my cock like a good little girl."

I was so close to coming I could barely breathe. His cock was like a fucking miracle wand hitting every sensitive and long-neglected spot inside of my raw and swollen pussy. I couldn't help but grind back against him.

"Yeah, that's it. Ride my fucking cock." He pulled out suddenly and dragged me all the way onto the bed. "Let's see how filthy you can get for me."

My legs were shaking as he towered over me. "Please… I need to cum."

A devious smirk played on his lips as he removed his shirt and pants, tossing them to the floor. "Play with yourself, darlin'. A good whore knows how to put on an even better show."

Fuck. I'd never been this bold in the bedroom before. Most of my sexual encounters were drunken, quick, and a blur that ended in me passing out with my panties still around my ankles. This was different.

I slid my fingers down my slit and rubbed my pussy lips back and forth. The heat in my body rose to inferno levels with each stroke. "Mmm…"

He watched me like he had the devil in his eyes. "Slide your finger inside that dirty cunt of yours. Push it in nice and deep."

I jerked my hips up as the pressure built in my core. As I pushed my finger all the way inside, I couldn't stop the agonizing moan that escaped from my throat.

Zander didn't take his eyes off my pussy as he shoved three thick fingers into my mouth. "That's a good girl."

He laughed again as I started to gag on him, which only made me hotter and needier for my climax. I ground against my own hand as he breathed heavily into my ear, "Cum for me, darlin'. Cum harder than any of your pencil-dick exes have ever made you cum."

An explosion of stars tunneled my vision at his lude command. I sucked his fingers like a lollipop as an earth-shattering orgasm rippled through me. He added his finger next to mine, shoving it just as deep inside my pussy. I bucked and jerked and trembled, spreading my thighs wide open to encourage the stretch.

"That's it beautiful, fucking just like that." He pressed his thumb hard against my clit as I hyperventilated into another orgasm. My body was not my own anymore. Zander had devastatingly possessed it with his lumberjack fucking hands and dirty fucking mouth.

When he removed his fingers from my mouth, I screamed out in a psychotic rage of chaos and desire and pure carnal lust. No man should be that good at this. It felt so fucking good, it made the ache in my chest grow even more.

And as he stilled his fingers inside my pussy, the most unexpected wave of emotions washed over me, and I started to cry.

"What the fuck?" Zander's eyes widened as he looked down at me. "Are you okay? Did I hurt you?"

I shook my head and curled up on my side. "No. I'm fine. I just want to be alone. Please leave."

He sighed. "Easton... did I do something wrong?"

Fuck. No, you did everything right. And that was the problem. I'm the one who's been doing everything wrong. But I couldn't voice anything coherent right now. "Get. The. Fuck. Out."

"Fuck. You really are an ice princess, aren't you?" He jumped off the bed. "It's no wonder you keep getting dumped."

I waited for him to slam the door behind him and listened to make sure his footsteps were far enough away before I let out the wail I'd been holding. Fuck. Zander was right. *I am an ice princess.* But whatever he just did to me was starting to thaw me out. And it fucking terrified me.

Chapter 6

EASTON

J slammed my laptop shut and screamed into my pillow. *Why am I fucking like this?*

The window rattled slightly as a flurry of fresh snow dusted it just as the lights flickered. *The storm's getting worse.* Great. I glared at my soiled yoga pants still lying on the floor and leaped off the bed. After rummaging around in my suitcase for ten minutes, I settled on a pair of silk drawstring pajama bottoms and a fresh tank top.

Satisfied that I didn't look like a harlot, I threw on my favorite pair of leather boots, *the one's that cost more than my condo in Florida,* and the one winter-*ish* coat I'd brought—well, it was a faux-fur duster, but it made me feel like the Viking princess from my last book.

Fuck, I was restless. Stir-crazy. There was only so much alone time I could have with myself after getting disgustingly and deliciously violated by a hot lumberjack-slash-possibly-fake innkeeper.

A wave of cringe washed over me again as I took a final glance around the garish room. *How the fuck am I supposed to sleep in this barrage of Christmas fuckery?*

I let out a dramatic sigh and marched downstairs. There was only one thing that might make me feel better about my life choices right now—ice cream and whiskey. Okay, that's two things but if I mixed them *together*… Oh, fuck a North Pole duck, I have more issues than this fucking inn.

The door off the dining room indeed led to the kitchen as I'd suspected earlier. I was relieved to find it empty and testosterone free. It didn't take me long to find the whiskey, which I promptly poured a double into the only cup I could find—a red mug with the words *Santa's Favorite Elf* etched across the front.

I rolled my eyes at it before I took a huge sip. Man, that old cat lady really loved Christmas. So fucking weird. The whiskey burned in the best way possible as it gushed down my throat. I almost did a little happy dance on my way to the fridge.

"Okay, what do we have here?" I muttered as I sifted through the packed freezer. There were multiple pints of ice cream—eggnog, candy cane, gingerbread, and pumpkin flavored. "Ugh," I grunted. "Where's the normal ice cream?" I just wanted chocolate or peanut butter, fuck, I'd even settle for plain old vanilla at this point.

"I thought you didn't *do* dairy," a smooth sexy voice chirped at me from behind.

I whipped around, startled, and fell back against the fridge. My breath hitched as I took in Penn's long muscled frame. I tried not to drool when my gaze landed on his soft thick kissable-looking lips. *Fucking Zander made me so horny I couldn't even look at any of them now without clenching my thighs.*

"Thanks for your concern, *Pencil*, but ice cream doesn't count," I snapped.

His eyes darkened as he stepped toward me, boxing me in against the fridge. He reached up and past me. I held my breath as he foraged around the freezer until a playful smirk spread across his lips. "Ah, here we go." He waved the pint of ice cream in front of my face. "The last pint of salted caramel."

My mouth instantly watered as I slid away from him and back against the center island. "You were hiding that, weren't you, Pencil?"

He snickered as he pulled two spoons out from one of the drawers. "If you behave, I'll let you have some. But call me Pencil one more time and I will tie you up and force you to watch me eat this entire pint by myself."

"Fine. *Penn.* May I please have some ice cream?" I should have just walked away but salted caramel was my favorite.

He winked and handed me a spoon. "Good girl."

Fuck. A spasm tickled my core. What was it about that phrase that turned my slut meter all the way up? *Keep your legs closed this time, Easton.* For fuck's sake.

As I dove for the pint with my spoon, Penn jerked it out of my reach. "On second thought, let's play a little game instead."

I sighed. "Seriously? It's late, I'm tired, and I just want a few bites before my brain explodes from Christmas hysteria."

Penn dipped his spoon into the pint, scooped up a heaping chunk of ice cream, and waved it in front of my face. "C'mon, beautiful, humor me."

My glands salivated as the spoon neared my lips. I could see the perfect glistening ribbons of caramel swirling in that luscious thick cream. I was half-tempted to snatch it from him and sprint up the stairs. But one look at the way his forearm flexed from his grip was enough of a warning. I was no match for him.

I threw my hands up in defeat. "What's the game?"

His grin widened. "I'll ask you a question about yourself and for every correct answer, you get a spoonful of ice cream."

I snickered. This idiot. Did he really think I was going to be honest? I'm a writer. It's literally my job to make up stories. "Deal."

He licked his lips. No, like literally and slowly dragged the tip of his tongue across his top and bottom lips like he was priming them for a meal. Fuck. There goes another spasm to my clit.

"And I'll know if you're lying, sweetheart. I'm good at a lot of things, but sniffing out a lie is my specialty," Penn drawled.

My stomach flipped. There was something about the way his shoulders pressed back as he said that. The way he looked me square in the eye with the confidence of an FBI interrogator. Fuck.

"Whatever. Let's just get this over with before the whole thing melts." I folded my arms and leaned back against the counter.

"Why are you here?"

"To finish my book."

Penn shook his head. "Nah. You can write a book anywhere. Why are you really *here*, Easton Radleigh?"

Ugh. I didn't even like talking to therapists about my life. "I needed somewhere quiet to get away and not be bothered. Clearly I failed on both accounts," I snarked.

Penn smirked. "Last chance to tell me the truth or face the consequences."

The ice cream was starting to drip off the spoon and onto the linoleum floor. I could just say fuck it and walk away. But something held me in place. A curiosity maybe. A pull to this gorgeous man who had every intention of pushing all of my buttons.

I wrapped my hand around his wrist and tugged the spoon toward my face. "Because even though I hate Christmas, I didn't want anyone to see me spending it alone. I came *here* because it seemed far enough away from the prying eyes of the press and paparazzi. I came to this god forsaken reindeer hell hole to finish my book in peace and not have to be reminded of how much I suck at love everywhere I look."

Penn nodded and slipped the spoon in my mouth. "Much better. Now you get a reward."

I practically came in my pants as the smooth buttery ice cream invaded my mouth. Fuck it was worth it.

He eyed my lips hungrily before removing the spoon. "Next question. Did you enjoy having Zander's cock inside you?"

Fuck me. My jaw dropped open. "What the fuck did you just say?"

Penn set the pint of ice cream down on the counter and

42

boxed me in with his Titan-looking arms. "You heard me. Well, I heard *you* to be exact. We all did. Your screams of ecstasy were… addicting. I'm only sad that I didn't get to watch."

What is happening?

I should be ashamed. Embarrassed. Outraged at his forwardness. But all I felt was complete and utter desire. "I… I don't know what you think you heard but—"

He pressed his finger to my lips. "Shhh. You don't have to be shy, darlin'. We're all friends here. And friends share everything."

Oh, fuck. He wants to fuck me too. Did I win the hot sex lottery? I couldn't really fuck two guys in one night, could I? "Um… thanks for the ice cream. I should get to bed."

Penn didn't move a muscle. "Take off your pants and get on the island."

I wrinkled my nose at him. "Are you stroking out? Please get out of my way."

His blue eyes lit up with amusement. "Have you ever had anyone lick ice cream off your pussy?"

Fuck. A lump formed in my throat. I could barely breathe, let alone speak. I just shook my head.

He untied my drawstring and my pajama bottoms fell to the floor. And now I wished I had put on a pair of panties.

Within seconds he was hoisting me up onto the center island. He chuckled as he yanked off my boots and finished pulling my pants completely off. "Lay back and spread your legs for me."

The counter was cold against my bare ass, but I did what he said. I didn't know what it was about these men, but I lost all fucking sense of reason and logic around them. *I was about to let a stranger eat me out.*

Penn retrieved the spoon and the pint of ice cream before circling back between my legs which were now spread eagle and dangling off either side of the island. "You're being such a good girl for me. And good girls get rewarded."

I shivered as he dropped a glop of ice cream onto my pussy. Oh, fuck. I could already feel it oozing down into my slit. "Fuck," I breathed.

He winked as he leaned over, his lips mere inches away from my clit. "Fuck, I love dessert."

I gasped and arched my back as he lashed his tongue up my slit, licking me from taint to clit. "Mmm, so fucking tasty." He puckered his lips around my nub, humming as he sucked.

I pulled at his silky blond strands as the pressure in my core increased. His tongue was firm and rough like sandpaper, and he knew exactly how to use it against all my most sensitive spots.

"Penn... oh my... fucking... god."

He peeled the lips of my pussy back with his sticky fingers and thrust his tongue deep inside. He darted in and out, gently scraping his teeth against my flesh in between soft sensual kisses.

I rolled my hips up and down as he devoured me, fucking his face like my life depended on it. I screamed as he nipped at my clit with his teeth while replacing his tongue with two thick fingers. He curved them up and pressed all the way back against my g-spot.

"Yeah, that's it. Grind that pussy on me. I want your cream all over my fingers," he growled.

Oh, fuck. Fuck. Fuck.

I needed more.

I pulled up my shirt, exposing my pebbled nipples. They were so swollen they hurt. I needed relief. I pinched them hard between my fingers.

Penn let out a low moan. "Oh, yeah, baby. Fuck. Show daddy how you like to touch yourself." He removed his fingers and grabbed the spoon. "I want another bite of your filthy cunt."

Fucking hell. I was done for. This man was about to do dirty fucking things to me. And I was going to let him.

Penn's eyes darkened as he rubbed the back of the spoon against my clit. "I want you to keep rubbing those nipples until they're raw."

I whimpered and bit down on my lip as he turned the spoon around and slid it down my slit and back up, working it back and forth. I arched up against it, urging him to keep going. "Harder," I moaned.

He pulled back and slapped my pussy hard with the spoon's cold metal back.

"Uhhh," I screamed. Fuck. I was so close. "I'm going to cum... fuck."

Penn chuckled and slapped me again before pulling my pussy lips back and massaging the spoon against my walls. "Fuck, yeah. Now that's the only cream I want to taste."

A deep spasm pierced through me as the last and final wave rushed in for the climax. I let out the loudest and deepest moan that I'd ever heard come out of me.

Penn rolled the spoon deep inside me as I came all over it.

"Ooh... fuck." He rubbed his thumb furiously over my clit as I rode out my orgasm. I writhed and thrashed on the counter as orgasm number two immediately followed.

As I panted in a pool of my own juices, I watched in awe as Penn shoved the cum covered spoon into his mouth and moaned. He closed his eyes and swallowed, pulling the spoon back out clean. "Delicious."

Chapter 7

EASTON

J couldn't get off that center island fast enough. Penn stared at me in amusement, that sloppy grin stretching across his face while I scrambled to get my pajama pants back on. I grabbed my glass of whiskey and waved my hand in his face. "Not a word about this to anyone. I'm going outside for some air. Do not follow me."

Penn choked back a laugh. "Outside? Honey, in case you haven't noticed, there's a wicked snowstorm happening out there."

I clenched my jaw, pursing my lips. "I'm not your honey. I'm a grown ass woman who needs some air."

He shrugged and stepped out of my way. "Oh, I forgot that ice princesses like snow. My bad... *honey.*"

Ugh. *What the fuck am I doing?* This trip was supposed to help me get away from men and sex and anything remotely love oriented. But here I was in the middle of nowhere with ice cream dripping out of my cunt while four of the sexiest men I'd ever seen wanted to take turns making me cum.

If this were a romance novel, I'd consider it a win, but it's my real fucking life and if anyone catches wind of what the fuck is going on here, my career and my reputation will be ruined.

I made my way to the back door of the inn and gave it three hard shoves before it finally opened. A chunk of snow fell from its frame and sprayed out around me, narrowly missing my head.

I closed my eyes and took a deep breath of icy air, relishing in the crisp chill that soothed my heated skin. I swirled the whiskey before taking a long sip. Mmm, that tasted even better after what Penn just did to my body. Fuck. It was like I no longer had a brain in my head. This place was turning me into a starved sex addict.

A loud bang sent a jolt of panic down my limbs. I jerked my head toward the noise, squinting through the thick snowfall to try and make out what it was. Fuck. Penn was right. *I shouldn't be out here.* A tiny light flickered a few feet away and I could make out the outline of a shed. Great. A snowstorm, four hot but mysterious guys, and a creepy shed. What could possibly go wrong?

I started to back up toward the door when I spotted Roman charging through the snow with two shovels. My fear turned to annoyance. *I can't get away from these guys.*

"Is that where you bury the bodies?" I snickered.

As he glanced up, a look of panic flickered in his eyes. But it disappeared and was quickly replaced with a warm smile. "Don't be silly. Everyone knows you don't bury the bodies at the scene of the crime."

My stomach knotted. He said that way too casually.

He burst out laughing. "Relax, Miss Radleigh. I just went to get some shovels to make sure the snow doesn't seal us all in. Fuck, you should have seen your face."

I let out a deep breath. "I knew that," I lied. "And call me Easton. Miss Radleigh makes me sound like my mother."

Roman nodded and licked his lips as he took stock of me. "You seem different. The boys get to you already?"

Fuck. Did he hear me moan too? "I don't know what you could possibly be talking about."

He threw down the shovels and pulled the collar of my coat up around my neck. "Let's get you inside before you catch a chill."

I was mesmerized by his brown eyes, his long thick lashes. I took another swig of my drink and let him lead me back inside. The lobby was so quiet you could hear a pin drop. With a loud grunt, Roman hoisted a pile of wood over to the fireplace and began piling it in.

I leaned against the front desk and watched the way his muscles flexed with each move he made. He smelled earthy and musky with a hint of something sweet like vanilla or maple. I wanted to rub my pussy against his stubbled chin so bad I could barely keep my knees from buckling. You couldn't get any manlier than him. He just built me a roaring fire for fuck's sake.

"You're awfully quiet for a change. Everything all right, Miss— er Easton?" His voice was gravelly despite his best efforts to keep it steady. There was an ache buried deep within. An ache that seemed to match mine.

"I'm just cold, that's all. Nothing to worry about," I lied.

He stretched his arm out toward me. "Come here. Let's get you warmed up."

Fuck. Here we go again.

I shrugged and shuffled over to him.

He eyed me like a wolf as he unbuttoned his flannel shirt and peeled it off. Tattoos covered every inch of his chiseled chest and stomach.

"Whoa, what are you doing?" My heart raced as I tried to look anywhere but at him.

He fingered the edges of my coat. "Body heat is the fastest way to get warm, darlin'. Let's get you out of these clothes so I can show you."

Oh, fuck. *I'm in my damn slut era, aren't I?* Nervous flutters shot through my stomach. "I fucked Zander and then let Penn eat my pussy," I blurted out.

Roman grinned. "I know. I heard you fucking Zander. And I saw you with Penn in the kitchen. It was hot watching you cum like that."

My cheeks flamed. "You-you just watched?"

He arched an eyebrow. "Were you hoping I would join? Well, I'm right here now, darlin'." He grabbed my chin and tugged it down, forcing my mouth to open, and pushed his thumb inside. "Take off your clothes and get on your knees in front of the fire."

I can't stop them. I don't want to.

With each touch, I was unraveling. No one had ever touched me like this. And now I had multiple men who could work miracles on my body. Is that what this was? A fucking Christmas sex miracle? *I'm either the luckiest woman in the world, or the stupidest.*

His eyes blazed with lust as I sucked his thumb. He pushed off my coat with his free hand. "I knew you'd be trouble the second you walked through that door, Easton Raleigh. The good fucking kind of trouble."

I whimpered as he pulled my tank top all the way down to my waist. "Fuck. I also knew you'd have the prettiest pink nipples." He rolled his thumb over each one and all the hairs on the back of my neck prickled. The pressure he applied was soft while the pads of his fingers were rough.

I released his thumb with a pop. "I don't usually do stuff like this…"

He wrapped his hand around my throat. "That's why you're wound so tight, darlin'. But I'm gonna get you nice and relaxed. Now take off your pajama bottoms so I can get a good long look at your sweet pussy."

My heart was bobbing between my throat and my stomach. I had just cum multiple times from two different dudes, but I was a greedy bitch and I wanted Roman to make me cum too. I was worse than an addict. I was a fiend.

With trembling fingers, I took off my boots and slid my pajamas down to my ankles. I rested my hand on Roman's shoulder as I stepped out of each leg.

"Turn around in a circle for me," he rasped.

I did so without hesitating, relishing in the fact that he was ogling my naked body like I was his to own.

"Good. Now get down on all fours."

I did, not caring if any of the others were watching. I secretly hoped they were. The bolder I got, the more depravity I craved.

He ran the tips of his fingers gently across my back. "Spread your legs farther apart."

As I widened my stance, my knees started to ache against the hard wooden floor. The pain only added to my arousal. "Roman…" I begged.

"Shhh. Relax." He walked behind me and slid his hands up the back of my thighs. "You look good on your knees. Good enough to eat."

My pulse kicked into high gear at the tickle of his fingertips sliding down my ass crack. "This is torture," I whispered.

He laughed. "I'm a masochist." He pulled my ass cheeks apart and I yelped as he pressed his hot tongue against my hole. He flicked the tip inside, sending shivers over every inch of me. No one had ever been back there before. No one.

"You like that. Good." He stood up again and walked around me twice more. "Let's see what else you like."

Before I could protest, he slid a black bag over my head. Panic spread through my veins. "Roman, I can't see. What the fuck?"

He rubbed my back gently. "That's the point, darlin'. Now get lower for me. Spread those legs wider."

As I lowered myself, spreading my legs as far as they'd go, my knees burned from digging into the wood. And then I felt the rope wrap around my wrists and tighten, binding them together. I tugged against them and began to thrash when I realized I couldn't get away. "*This hurts*, Roman," I whimpered.

"Shh. The pleasure will be worth the pain." He shoved my head down to the floor, holding it firmly in place with one hand while grabbing a fistful of my ass with the other. "You're a feral animal, Easton. Like a wild horse that needs to be broken."

He wedged a thick finger inside my asshole, sending a deep spasm of pleasure to my core. He pumped it in and out slowly while shoving another finger inside my pussy. "You look like a filthy fucking whore. So fucking sexy. You're taking it so well for me."

I couldn't see what was happening. My wrists and knees were no doubt marked and bruised. I couldn't scream for help even if I wanted to. And a part of me wanted to. But not because I was scared of Roman. It was because I was scared of myself. This fantasy I had... it was wrong and sick. "Let me go. I don't want to do this anymore."

I bucked as a hard slap came down on my ass and his fingers inched deeper inside both of my holes. My clit throbbed with need and ache. "But you're so fucking wet, darlin'. And I'm just getting started."

Oh, dear god. *What have I gotten myself into?*

Another slap came down against my tender flesh, but the stinging only made my clit throb for more. "I've been wanting to teach you a lesson ever since you opened your filthy mouth."

I moaned at his words. *Why is this turning me on?*

"Mmm, still want me to stop, darlin'?" he asked as he see-sawed his fingers back and forth between my ass and my pussy.

My body was shaking, trembling, sweating with pure carnal lust. I was about to collapse. "Fuck... I can't... I don't... know."

Without warning, he withdrew his fingers, untied my ropes, and ripped the bag off of my head. "Get on your back."

I flipped over, grateful to have the pressure off my knees. My belly knotted as I looked up to see the crazed look in his eyes, the menacing snarl on his lips. "Please..."

"Are you begging me to stop or to keep going?"

My heart raced as I watched him unbutton his jeans and slide them off, my eyes widening as I drank in the sight of his massive, tattooed cock. "I-I don't know." I did know. I wanted that beautiful cock inside me so bad I could hardly stand it. But saying it out loud would truly make me their whore. And I wasn't sure if I was ready for that.

He smirked and lowered himself between my legs. He grabbed the tip of his cock and rubbed it slowly up and down my slit. "I'm going to fuck you either way, darlin', but I want to hear you beg. No matter what it's for."

"I-I thought you were the nice one..." I was shocked at the turn of events. Roman was the last person in this inn that I expected to be the brutal one.

He stroked himself as he pushed his cock another inch inside my pussy. "Oh, I can be very nice when it's deserving. But not to spoiled brats who think they're better than everyone."

I gasped at his words. "You don't understand. I'm not a brat... I just..." It was getting harder to speak with the girth of his cock stretching me open.

He rubbed his thumb in circles around my clit. "Beg like a good little whore and I might change my mind about you."

I whimpered. "Please..."

He slapped the inside of my thigh. "Please what?" He inched his cock in farther but kept it still. It was fucking agonizing.

"Please. Fuck. Me." I closed my eyes and bit down on my lower lip.

He slapped my thigh again. "Look at me."

I opened my eyes and took a deep breath.

"Yeah, that's a good girl. You keep your eyes on me until I tell you to look away." He let out a deep moan as he pushed all the way inside my pussy.

I cried out as his thickness pulsed against my insides, sending tingles to every inch of my core.

He plunged deeper in before pulling out and thrusting back in with more force. "Gag yourself for me."

My pulse quickened. "What?"

He pounded into me so hard, my body slid a few inches across the floor. "Stick two fingers in your mouth and fucking gag yourself."

This sent another spasm to my aching clit. I opened my mouth wide and inserted two fingers. This was fucking hot. I couldn't deny it.

"Mmm, fuck. I knew you were a dirty girl but damn, baby, you're fucking filthy."

I was swept up in his brutal rhythm, his foul words, and his delicious pain. I pushed my fingers down my throat, desperate to please him. And I made myself actually gag. Tears streamed down my cheeks.

"Yeah, choke for me. So fucking beautiful." He wrapped his hand around my throat and squeezed as my body convulsed. His cock swelled inside my pussy right before a burst of thick hot cum filled me.

He cried out, his voice almost demonic, as he slammed into

me over and over again. My spasms quickened until they merged into one final explosion, taking over every inch of me. I screamed as the sudden rush of my orgasm took over.

"That's it. Cum for daddy. Soak my fucking cock with your filthy cream," he growled.

This was some next level degradation. With my fingers still in my throat and our eyes locked, I came two more times on his thick cock. Each veiny ridge felt like heaven sliding against my tender flesh.

I couldn't catch my breath even as he stilled. "Holy...fuck."

"There ain't nothing holy about what we just did, darlin'." He pulled his cock out and stood up, towering over me. "But I never considered myself a holy man."

I eyed him carefully. The feral look had mostly left his gaze, but it was still there, simmering just below the surface. *This man is a fucking beast.*

"You okay?" he asked, breathless.

I shook my head. "I think you and your friends ruined sex with other people for me."

He smirked. "Nah. We just gave you better standards."

Chapter 8

VANCE

burst of blood sprayed out as my fist connected with the fake innkeeper's nose. Yeah, we weren't the only ones pretending this weekend. We followed this sick fuck all the way to the town that God forgot, but we were too late. He'd already offed the nice little cat lady and stuffed her into the walk-in freezer.

"Did you think you could hide from us forever?" I roared into his face.

He whimpered and looked down at his soiled crotch.

I slapped him across the face like the little bitch he was. "You got some balls thinking you could get away with what you did to all those women. But you really fucked up when you fucked with our boss's daughter. Ooh, doggie. Tell me, asshole, did you have any idea who you were messing with in the club that night?"

"Please," the douchebag pleaded, "I didn't know. I'm sorry."

I grabbed a pair of pliers and positioned them over his hand.
"That poor girl will be in therapy for the rest of her fucking life after
what you did. But you know what we really came here for. Where
is it?"

He shook his head, sniveling like a child. "I don't have it. I
swear."

I sighed in annoyance. They always tried to play dumb until
they realized I didn't fuck around. If they were honest right away,
I might go easier on them... But not this fucker. Nah. He's a real
fucking piece of shit.

"Liar." I grabbed his hand and in one quick jerk, pulled off the
nail of his index finger with the pliers.

He let out a bloodcurdling scream. Luckily for us, I sound-
proofed the basement earlier. By myself, I might add, since Zander,
Penn, and Roman were too busy catching feelings for our unwanted
guest. Don't get me wrong, Easton Radleigh was hot as fuck. But
she didn't pay our bills. Though, this motherfucker right here was
about to.

"Imma ask you again before I separate you from another part
of your body. Where is the money you stole?"

A fresh stream of piss whizzed out from between his legs and
onto the cement floor. He shook his head. "It's gone. I already spent
it. Fuck."

I knelt down and jabbed the pliers into his thigh. "Oh, yeah?
What did you spend it on? Drugs? Hookers? Fucking diapers for
your little bladder problem?"

He let out another scream as I dug the tip of the pliers deep into his flesh. "I bet I could hit an artery with my eyes closed. Fucking talk."

"I-I had debts. The money's gone. I swear."

This motherfucker was telling the truth. I let out a dramatic sigh before moving the pliers from his thigh back to his hand. "Well, seems you got a new debt. *To us.* Imma take the first payment right now."

The sound of him screaming got my dick hard as I pulled the rest of his fingernails off, one by one. If it was anyone else, I might feel bad… but this abomination of a man hurt women. Like really fucking hurt them in ways that you don't even want to think about. So I enjoyed torturing him a little extra.

As I turned to head back upstairs, a loud crack rang through the air just before everything went pitch black. Fuck. The storm must be getting worse if it knocked out the fucking power.

I flicked open my zippo lighter and started searching for the fuse box.

The minutes were ticking by as I scoured through every corner and crevice of this musty basement. My patience was waning fast. I was getting sick of listening to that piece of shit cry and whimper. I was tempted to knock him out just to shut him up. But that would bring him relief and that's the last thing that prick deserved. Nah. I wanted him to suffer. So I had to suffer too apparently.

Suddenly the door at the top of the stairs creaked open, followed by the clicking sound of heels, and my stomach dropped. Fuck. Unless Zander, Penn, or Roman got a sudden penchant for dressing up in women's clothing, that sound could only mean one thing… The fucking ice princess found the basement.

Fuck.

I darted over to the hostage and closed my hand around his mouth. "Don't make one fucking sound or I'll gut you open right fucking now," I whispered.

I felt him nod his head in the dark. Now I just needed to keep my pulse and breath under control, and hope that Easton didn't realize we were down here.

"Hello?" She called out. "Is anyone down here?" She cursed under her breath as what sounded like her fumbling the last few steps echoed through the room. "Fuck. I swear I heard voices down here," she muttered.

My heart raced as a whiff of her perfume tickled my nose. Fuck she smelled good. Ugh. *Just go back upstairs you nosy brat.*

She cursed again as her footsteps moved away from us, back toward the stairs. I almost let out a sigh of relief when the fixture above me buzzed and snapped... and the fucking lights came back on.

As her gaze traveled from my eyes all the way down to my bloodied hand and the asshole I had in an iron grip, she let out a bloodcurdling scream that would rival any horror movie queen.

Chapter 9

EASTON

Every fear and nightmare I've had since arriving at the Briar patch was coming true. I was alone in the middle of a snowstorm with four serial killers. Fuck.

I backed up toward the stairs slowly. "Please don't hurt me."

Vance snickered and stepped away from the bloodied man he had tied to a chair. "Relax, darlin'. I'm not gonna hurt you. Just stay calm. This isn't what it looks like."

What the actual fuck? My adrenaline spiked in my veins as nausea crept up my throat. "Well it very much looks like you've been torturing this man to death. Am I next?"

He inched forward, wiping the sweat off his brow with his beautiful forearm. His thick, muscled, tattooed forearm. "He's a very bad man, Easton. I have my reasons. Reasons you could never even imagine."

Something about the way he looked at me was turning me on. *No, Easton. Bad girl.* "Are you gonna kill him? And then kill me next? I know I haven't been very nice to you, but I don't deserve to die."

He smirked and his eyes lit up. "Oh, no? What else did you have in mind?"

Fuck. My hands trembled as I reached back for the railing. Maybe I could make it up there in time. Maybe I could get away…

"He's a maniac," the bound man screamed. "Help me, please."

Vance slapped the man across the face. "You shut the fuck up. Ain't no one helping you."

I whimpered and leaped back. "What is wrong with you? You're all a bunch of monsters."

Vance sighed. "No we're on a job. And this piece of shit doesn't deserve your sympathy." I tugged on his ear. "Isn't that right, sicko? I bet you're thinking of all the disgusting things you'd do to my friend here if you weren't tied up."

The man sneered back at him. "She'd look so pretty in a cage."

My stomach knotted and I almost gagged on my own bile. I swallowed hard, forcing it back down. Chills swept across my skin. "Vance? What's going on?"

Vance walked over to me and caressed my cheek. "It's nothing for you to worry about. Now go back upstairs and wait for me, beautiful."

My breath hitched in my throat as I stared deep into his light green eyes. He was so fucking handsome it hurt to look at him. "Are you going to be okay?"

He arched an eyebrow. "You concerned about someone other than yourself? I'm impressed. The boys really did a number on you."

I felt my cheeks flush. Fuck. "You four don't keep any secrets from each other, do you?"

A devious glint sparked in his eye. "We don't keep *anything* from each other."

I backed up against the wall with a sudden need for this man to touch me. The ache stirred in my pussy like a drug. *Why am I like this?* There's a man beaten and bleeding just a few feet away from me and all I could think about was Vance's hands on me.

"Oh, you are into some freaky shit, aren't you," Vance drawled. He pressed up against me and nipped at my neck. "You want me to make you cum right here?"

I swallowed hard and nodded, afraid to use my words.

He chuckled and slipped his hand down my pants. "Mmm, you're so fucking wet. Your pussy likes danger. That makes me so hard."

I let out a moan as he wedged a finger deep inside my cunt. He slid it in and out slowly as he kissed my neck. "Vance... fuck. That feels so good."

He growled and added a second finger while he wrapped his other hand around my throat. "You want me to fuck you against this wall, beautiful?"

I moaned again. "Yes, please... I need you inside me." I glanced over his shoulder to see their deranged hostage watching us, aroused. And it made me wetter. A devious idea formed in my head.

Vance unbuckled his belt and slid it out of the loops. "I'm going to fill you with so much cum you won't be able to walk for a week without dripping it everywhere you go."

I kissed him hard on the lips, gasping as our tongues met and twirled around each other in a desperate frenzy. "Vance... I want you to fuck me where he can see."

He stilled and looked down at me, a fresh smirk playing across his lips. "Dirty girl. I had you figured all wrong. I like this side of you, darlin.'"

In one quick move, Vance swooped me up and set me on the workshop table, directly across from his hostage. He yanked off my pants and tossed them to the floor. "Open your legs so I can see how your pussy glistens for me."

I arched my back and spread my legs open. "I lied earlier," I breathed.

Vance lined his cock up to my entrance. "About what exactly?"

It was my turn to smirk. "I loved it when you called me baby."

"Fuck, yeah." He plunged his cock deep inside without any coaxing, burrowing himself to the hilt. He swelled and throbbed against my walls, and it felt like I was on fucking fire.

Fuck, this man was an angel and the devil all in one. "Yes," I cried out. "Harder. Fuck me harder."

And he did.

I flung my head to the side to look at the hostage. "Guess I'm good at torturing people too. That asshole wants to touch himself so bad."

Vance laughed. "You might be more sadistic than me, darlin'. I fucking love that about you." He rolled his hips into mine and thrust his cock slowly in and out so I could feel each magical ridge against my swollen pussy.

My clit spasmed as waves of ecstasy fluttered through me. I cried out, scratching and clawing at his back as my orgasm threatened to steal my last breath. Stars exploded in my vision as his hand tightened around my neck, cutting off my oxygen. The pressure in my core was almost unbearable in the best possible way.

As he released his hold on my throat, I felt the rush of his hot cum filling my insides and it triggered another orgasm. "Oh, baby. Mmm… Merry. Fucking. Christmas."

We rocked against each other like wild animals, clinging to each other for dear life, before collapsing together in a heap of sweat and cum.

"For fuck's sake, Vance, she knows everything now," Roman chided, his voice breaking through the stillness of the basement.

I looked up to see him, Zander, and Penn standing at the foot of the stairs, their faces a mixture of lust and annoyance. "Hi, guys."

Vance climbed off of me and pulled up his pants. "She came down here when the power went out. What was I supposed to do? Off her?"

Zander snickered. "You fucking *offed* her all right… She knows our names and our faces. We can't exactly just let her go."

Penn nodded. "He's right. I know she's not our usual mark, but she knows way too much."

I yanked my pants back up and threw my hands in the air. "Hello? *She* is still in the room. I'm not going to tell anyone about… this." I pointed toward the hostage.

Roman threw me a pained look. "We don't know that for sure. How can we trust you?"

My head was buzzing from the multiple orgasms I'd just had and the possible threat to my life if I didn't think of something fast. I looked back and forth between them and their hostage. Fuck.

My hands trembled as I picked up a wrench from the workshop table. As I staggered over to the man tied up in the chair, his eyes widened. He shook his head. "What-what are you doing?"

Fuck. Fuck. *What am I doing?* But there was no other way to get out of this.

"Sealing my fate." I took a deep breath and swung the wrench as hard as I could against his knee.

The man screamed in agony as his leg contorted.

I turned around to see all four of my Christmas psychos staring back at me with wide eyes, their mouths agape.

The wrench made a loud clank as I let it fall to the floor. "That makes me an accomplice. Do you trust me now?"

Chapter 10

EASTON

I sat on the glitter-bombed couch in the lobby across from the front desk with a fuzzy reindeer blanket wrapped around my shoulders. Penn handed me a cup of hot cocoa right after Vance spiked it with whiskey. As I took a sip, a shudder ran through me, followed by a spark of excitement. I should have been horrified but all I could think about was the rush of adrenaline that was still pumping through my veins. And the fact that I finally knew how I was going to finish my book.

The grandfather clock chimed, causing us all to flinch. "It's midnight," Roman announced.

I held my nose over my steaming cup of boozy hot cocoa. "It's Christmas."

Zander took a seat next to me. "You didn't have to do what you did downstairs."

I snickered. "Didn't I?"

"We weren't going to hurt you, Easton," Penn added.

"Oh, now you tell me. Thanks. Excuse me if I didn't want to end up tied to a chair next to that pervert." I gulped down a huge sip of my drink, praying that the buzz kicked in sooner rather than later. As I looked around the room at the twinkling lights from the three gaudy Christmas trees, my stomach lurched. "Now what?"

Roman wiped the sweat from his face with the back of his hand, exhaustion creeping into his eyes. "That's up to you, princess. You can call the cops, tell them everything... we won't stop you."

My heart raced. Tell them what? That I fucked four criminals in between them beating the shit out of a man in the basement? That I enjoyed every single second of it? *Every earth-shattering orgasm they gave me.*

"Or," Vance chimed in, "you could give us a head start to get away. We're good at disappearing."

Well, fuck. I didn't really like that scenario either. Was I foolish to think that I could actually continue a relationship with all four of them after tonight? Or that they would want to too?

I blew out a deep breath. "Were you telling the truth about that man down there? Did he really do all that weird shit to women?"

The four of them nodded in unison. "Full disclosure, that's *not* why we came after him," Roman rasped, "but yeah, he's a monster."

"So, it just made beating him within an inch of his life that much easier," Zander added.

A warm fuzzy feeling stirred in my belly. "Then you are doing the world a favor. I can't turn you in." I took another sip of my cocoa while they held their breaths, waiting for me to explain. "I'm not going to give you a head start… I'm letting you go. I'll call the police as soon as you're gone. I'll tell them that when I checked in, that asshole held me hostage and that I spent all night trying to get away. You'll need to knock him out and untie him so it's somewhat believable."

Penn's eyes widened. "You'd take the fall for us?"

I snickered. "It was self-defense, right? Besides… I'm not as selfish as you all think I am."

Zander grabbed my hand and gave it a light squeeze. "Are you sure? They're going to ask you a lot of questions… And because of who you are, this will be all over the news so fast it will make your head spin."

My stomach knotted. "I know."

"The press will make your life a living hell," Roman added.

"They already make my life a living hell. I knew what I was signing up for when I decided to become an author."

Vance nodded. "But once that guy's rap sheet comes out, you'll be a hero to women everywhere."

I shrugged. "That's not why I'm doing this."

"Why are you really doing this?" Roman asked.

I wrang my hands together nervously, suddenly shy around these beautiful psychos. "Because I arrived here as an uptight, bitter woman with zero interest in letting myself experience any kind of joy. But you… In just one night, you four have made me feel a fire I've never felt before. And I don't want to be an ice princess anymore."

Penn winked. "Your body felt nice and warm to me, darlin'. Looks like we thawed you out."

I took one look at his tousled hair and sloppy grin and couldn't help but burst out laughing. "I've been a massive slut this weekend, haven't I?"

Vance cupped my chin in his hand, tilting it up as he looked down at me hungrily. "You're *our* slut."

My pussy tingled under his gaze. I was starring in my very own romance novel, and I didn't want it to end. But it had to... So I needed one last memory before letting them walk away from me forever.

I stood up and walked over to the candy-cane lined staircase. I threw them the most seductive look I could muster. "Wait ten minutes and then come up to my room."

As I lay on the bed naked, tangled up in multiple strings of colorful Christmas lights, I almost lost my nerve. The old Easton would have settled for a quickie in between publicity events. The me I was before arriving at the Briar Patch only dated passionless men with zero charm. Despite the fact that Zander, Roman, Penn, and Vance were criminals, they had been the most chivalrous men I'd ever met. And they'd made me cum more times tonight than I'd had all year.

My breath hitched as all four of them entered my room. I took notice of their eyes, the way they lit up like Christmas trees at the sight of me. "Too much?" I squeaked out.

Zander shook his head as he stalked over to the bed. He

grabbed my wrist and used one end of the lights to secure it to the bed post. My pulse raced as he did the same to my other wrist. "Now you're just right."

Moisture pooled between my thighs as Vance settled in next to me on the bed. Roman nestled in between my legs, softly caressing my thighs. And Penn cozied up to Zander on the other side. They were practically salivating as they eyed me like a Christmas buffet.

Vance pushed his thumb into my mouth. I moaned as I sucked, swirling my tongue in circles around it. "Ooh, baby. You're in trouble now."

Trouble is exactly what I need.

Zander pinched one of my nipples between his fingers while Penn covered the other one with his soft wet lips. I arched my back, urging them to keep going. "Mmm, fuck. Do whatever you want to me…"

Roman growled as he pressed my thighs back against the mattress. He hollowed his cheeks and puckered his lips before releasing a thick glob of saliva onto my pussy. I gasped as it dripped down my slit. He used his index finger to smear it all over my folds.

Zander nipped at my earlobe. "Are you our dirty girl?"

I nodded, whimpering. "Yes…"

"She's so fucking wet," Roman rasped. "You gonna be a good girl and take all of us?"

I could barely breathe. All I could do was nod.

Roman fisted his cock, lining it up at my entrance. The ache in my core festered as he teased me. "Please…"

Vance reached over and pulled my pussy lips back, spreading

me wide for Roman's thick cock. "Go slow so we can see her pussy swallow every inch."

I cried out as he slid in slowly. Zander and Penn sucked on my nipples so hard I thought they might burst. But the pressure felt so fucking good.

I rolled my hips up as Roman burrowed himself all the way in. Vance wrapped his hand around the base of Roman's cock while keeping a thumb firmly pressed against my clit. "Yeah just like that, baby. Lift up and down."

He fucked me hard while Vance guided him in and out of my pussy. It was the most erotic thing I'd ever felt. Watching his hand slide up and down Roman's cock as it entered me… I screamed as an orgasm rippled through me without warning.

Roman grunted as he pounded into me. "Fuck, I can't hold it." His cum shot forward, filling me so full, it leaked out all over Vance's hand.

The second he pulled out, Zander untied my wrists and flipped me over onto my stomach. He yanked my hips back and thrust his cock deep inside me. "Damn, it's like a fucking oven in here." He pumped in and out, sending deep spasms to my core. "Sticky too. Mmm…"

Penn grabbed a fistful of my hair and jerked my head up. "Let's get this mouth nice and sticky too." Without warning, he shoved his cock into my mouth. I moaned as I tasted his pre cum mixed with his salty sweat. "Fuck, you're taking me so fucking well." He rammed the back of my throat and I gagged but that didn't stop him. Tears streamed down my cheeks as he punished my mouth while Zander fucked me from behind. They pushed and pulled me back and forth between them while Roman and Vance took turns stroking my clit.

I felt like I was going to explode into a thousand pieces. But I didn't want it to stop. They were worshiping me and punishing me all at the same time. I didn't even know this was what I'd been craving all along.

Zander roared like a beast as he unleashed a thick burst of cum inside my swollen pussy. He slapped my ass cheeks as he came. "Such. A. Dirty. Fucking. Whore."

Another wave of spasms rolled through me as I ground against his dick, twisting, and turning under Roman and Vance's fingers on my nub. It was the final push over the edge. My scream was stifled by Penn unloading his hot cum inside my mouth.

As Roman and Vance licked the cum off my thighs, I swallowed every drop of Penn. "That's my little Christmas angel, drinking her milk like a good little girl." I sucked harder as his filthy words turned me on even more. I whimpered at the pull of his hands tangled in my hair... he was so deep inside my throat, I was starting to see stars.

When he finally pulled out, I gasped for air. "I want more."

"Insatiable, aren't you? Don't worry, princess. We ain't done with you yet," Zander drawled.

Vance switched places with Zander. He dragged a finger down my ass crack. "I want this tight little hole."

My ass literally puckered at the thought of his huge cock entering my tiny vulnerable space. "Um... I've never done that before."

He snickered. "We better get you nice and lubed up then."

Vance gently pulled my ass cheeks apart and spit inside of me. I shuddered and my toes curled as it tickled me in a way that felt so good I could have cried. He chuckled at my reaction before slipping his tongue inside my ass hole.

I clenched and bucked. "Holy fuck!"

"Shh relax, darlin," Roman cooed as he rubbed my nipples.

Penn stroked my clit. "Yeah, the more you relax, the better it will feel."

Oh, fuck. This was intense.

Vance moaned as he devoured me. When he came up for air, he replaced his tongue with two fingers. I yelped as he stretched me. "There we go, now you're starting to open up for me." He added a third finger just as Zander lobbed a glob of spit down my slit. "That should help."

"Ooh yeah, that's slipping in nicely."

I couldn't help but grind against his hand. This felt wild and dark and wrong and so fucking right all at the same time. The pressure in my ass made my pussy tingle so much that I almost blacked out when Roman and Penn each shoved a finger inside it.

Vance moaned as my juices poured out. "Mmm. Let's fucking go." He inched the tip of his cock into my ass, and I screamed. "Ooh, baby girl. You're so fucking tight. Oh my god." He slid in farther and I arched back, my legs shaking uncontrollably. Roman and Penn took turns pumping their fingers in and out of my pussy.

"Let me in, darlin'," Vance rasped. He spread my ass cheeks apart with his calloused hands and forced his cock all the way in. It felt like I was being ripped open. My insides were on fire. A blood-curdling scream erupted from my throat. But within seconds, I felt a pleasure deep in my core that was new to me. Sensations I could never even imagine. *Why have I never done this before?*

I moaned loud and deep as he rode me. "Oh, shit. Don't stop."

Vance growled, "Mmm, I'm not going anywhere, baby."

He increased his speed and force as I stretched around him. And when his cum entered my ass, it made my whole body shake with pleasure so hard I collapsed onto my stomach. Roman and Penn kept their fingers in my pussy, stroking me while I rode it out, while Zander slapped my ass raw as Vance unleashed everything he had inside me.

Merry fucking Christmas indeed.

Chapter 11

EASTON

J stood at the window and watched the snow melt as the sun began to rise. A flurry of emotions took hold of me as I reflected on the past twenty-four hours—the most sinful night of my life. It was my awakening. In Roman, Zander, Penn, and Vance, I found a sexual freedom that I'd lost a long time ago. For that, I'd be forever grateful to them. But it was bittersweet. In order to give them *their* freedom, I had to let them go.

Roman took my clammy hands in his. "You sure you wanna do this, darlin'?"

I forced back a nervous laugh. It was the only thing I was sure of. "How could I send you all to prison when you broke me out of mine?"

Zander held out his hand and I almost doubled over laughing

when I saw the half-smoked cigar. "I want you to have it. You're one of us now."

I took the cigar, my heart swelling with so much affection for these guys. "Thank you, Zander. I'll make sure to savor it slowly and think of you with every puff."

Next came Penn, who sheepishly shuffled over to me with the infamous pint of salted caramel in his hands. "You should finish this before the cops raid the place. I know it's your favorite."

"Thanks *Penn.*"

His eyes lit up. "Fuck it. Call me Pencil. It kind of turns me on."

We all burst out laughing. Except for Vance.

He pulled me into an embrace. His breath was hot and erratic in my ear. "Come find us someday, baby girl."

I choked back a sob that I wasn't expecting. I'd grown attached to these brutes in such a short time. It was starting to make me physically ache at the thought of letting them walk out the door.

I threw my arms around his neck and squeezed him with all my strength. "Leave a trail of breadcrumbs for me," I whispered back.

"The storm's breaking which means the town will be buzzing to life soon," Roman quipped. "We need to leave now if we don't want to get caught."

My stomach knotted. "He's right. You need to go… Be safe out there."

Vance chuckled. "Yeah we don't want to be late for our *Only Fans* meeting."

I couldn't help but giggle at that. "Fuck, I was such a brat, wasn't I?"

Zander ran his thumb across my lower lip. "You take care of yourself, princess."

I nodded, fighting back the tears and emotions I wasn't prepared to feel.

"The truck's gassed up and ready to go, boys," Penn rasped. He planted a soft kiss on my cheek before heading to the door.

I wanted to cry out for them. I wanted to beg them to stay. Or beg them to take me with them. But I had to stick to the plan so we could all get away. So, I just stood there and watched them leave. I tried to tell myself that they weren't longing for me too. That it pained them just as much to leave me behind. I had to toughen up that outer shell again otherwise I'd collapse into a sniveling mess. And I definitely didn't want to lose my dignity in the middle of the inn that murdered Christmas. I waited until they were gone for at least an hour before I picked up the front desk phone and dialed 911.

This was worse than I'd imagined. Where did all these people come from?

It was as if the entire town had moved back overnight and camped out on the front steps of the Briar Patch Inn. I was suffocating in a sea of camera bulbs, flashing police lights, and bystanders snapping pics of me with their phones.

I could see the headline now: *Romance author Easton Radleigh is so lonely she gets herself kidnapped and held hostage on Christmas.*

"Ma'am, can you please tell us again what happened? That man is badly beaten, and you don't have a scratch on you." The handsome police officer with the candy cane tattoo—*what in the actual fuck was wrong with this town?* —wanted to believe me, but he also wanted to believe that Santa Claus was real. Both were untrue.

I sighed and gave my best helpless victim impression. "I guess my adrenaline took over, officer. I was fighting for my life. Sadly, the old lady wasn't so lucky."

His partner walked up and threw him a puzzled look. "The perp is on three different watchlists. The FBI, CIA, and DEA all want his ass." The second officer turned to me. "Looks like you deserve a medal. They've been trying to catch this creep for years."

I nodded and tried my best to hide my grin. My guys caught him. Three different government agencies let that asshole slip through their fingers, but he couldn't get away from Roman, Penn, Zander, or Vance.

"I-I was just so scared he was going to kill me. I didn't even know my own strength," I whimpered.

The first officer arched an eyebrow at me but conceded. He knew this was a mystery he'd never solve. So he took the win. "Well, stranger things have happened. You're free to go now, Miss Radleigh. But we'll be in touch if we have more questions."

I didn't blow out a sigh of relief until I was in the Uber halfway to the airport. I fished around for my flask and took a big sip. The driver eyed me in the rearview mirror.

Ugh. Here we go again. "It's whiskey. You want some?"

He gasped. "I'm driving."

I shrugged. "Suit yourself."

When we pulled up to my gate, the driver couldn't get me and my luggage out the door fast enough. "Merry Christmas," I called back condescendingly. Fucking hell I forgot how annoying and *judgey* the general population could be.

I was already dreading my flight home. But the thought of walking into my empty condo disturbed me more. Two days ago, being alone was my favorite thing. Now that I had a taste of the most erotic sex of my life... that was my new favorite thing. Them.

I downed the rest of my whiskey before tossing the flask in the trash. I'd get another one on the other side when I landed.

As I approached the check-in desk, a loud voice blared over the PA system, "Easton Radleigh, please make your way over to the jet center." The message repeated three more times. *What the fuck?*

I turned on my phone and instantly wished that I hadn't. SEVEN HUNDRED NOTIFICATIONS. Fuck me. I wished I hadn't gotten rid of my flask. Ugh. My publicist must have booked me a private jet because of all of the bad press. *So much for me having an anonymous trip to the country.*

As I charged through the airport in search of the jet center, I did my best to avoid the stares and snickers from everyone I passed. *I bet Stephen King doesn't have to deal with this bullshit. Fuck.*

A pretty blonde opened the glass door for me as soon as I approached. "Miss Radleigh, welcome. Your jet is fueled and ready to go. Follow me."

I let her take my bags as I hurried to catch up with her on the tarmac. "Um, are you sure this is for me? I already have a ticket for another flight."

She smiled warmly over shoulder. "Oh, yes. Don't worry we refunded that for you. Now watch your step."

My dread and confusion was growing with each step I took

up the airstair. I was greeted by another flight attendant at the top, a short dark haired man. He handed me a glass of champagne. "They're waiting for you."

What? Oh, fuck. As I walked into the main cabin, my stomach flipped. Roman, Zander, Penn, and Vance lounged casually in their seats, looking like they really were heading to an Only Fans meeting. They were gorgeous. Like unnaturally stunning.

My breath hitched. "You waited for me?"

Roman patted the seat next to him. "Of course, darlin'. We ain't going anywhere without our ice princess."

I was speechless. For the first time. Ever. No quippy comeback. Just shock and awe.

Zander laughed. "We figured you could finish your book in Cabo."

"I'm sure we could find lots of ways to *inspire* you," Penn added.

My heart fluttered as I looked at Vance for confirmation. He was the grumpiest of the four so if he said it too… then it must be real. He winked back at me. "I figured we'd find you first, baby."

I let out the deep breath I'd been holding and gave each of them a kiss before taking my seat. They were my four gifts wrapped in charm and psychotic tendencies. So, maybe I didn't hate Christmas after all.

Roman squeezed my knee as the jet began to move on the tarmac. "Cabo it is then?"

I smirked as a rush of adrenaline spiked in my veins. "I just need to make one stop first."

They each threw me an expectant look. "Oh, yeah?" Zander asked. "Where to?"

"To go crash a book club party." I grinned as I imagined the look on Betty's face when I rolled up with these four. "How do you all feel about Viking costumes?"

The five of us burst out laughing as the jet lifted off. I didn't care about the headlines anymore. Fuck what anyone thought of me. I was finally living my best life, full of adventure and romance and spontaneity. The kind of life that I wrote about in my books. Except now I was the main character. Call it fate, free-will, or a fucking Christmas miracle, but I, Easton Radleigh am finally writing my own happy ending.

More books by
M VIOLET

Pretty Little Psycho (The Devils of Raven's Gate Book 1)

Good Girl (Wickford Hollow Duet Book 1)

Little Fox (Wickford Hollow Duet Book 2)

Wickford Hollow Duet (includes Good Girl, Little Fox, and an exclusive bonus chapter of Riot and Maureen)

Wicked Midnight
(A Dark Why Choose Romance Retelling of Cinderella)

Acknowledgements

Happy Holidays! Thank you for reading my dirty little Christmas novella. I had so much fun writing it.

Thank you to my Street Team and ARC teams! You have been with me since the beginning and there aren't enough words to express how much I love you. Thank you for being on this journey with me.

Thank you to my all my Vixens! Your love and support continues to warm my dark little heart. I am so lucky to have the best readers an author could ask for.

Thank you to my amazing PA, Darcy Bennett, for everything you do. You support me in my chaos, and I would be lost without you in this crazy world of publishing. YOU ARE A SAINT.

Thank you to my girls in the Smutven! I love each and every one of you so much. Your daily chats, memes, advice, and support give me life! I can't wait to party with you all in person. XOXO

To my girl Cara/Cassie, I am so proud of everything you've accomplished. I am so thankful and grateful to have you in my life. We truly are soul sisters. Love you!

Thank you to all my family and friends. You know who you are. XOXO

Thank you Stacey Blake for your talent, friendship, and support. I would literally be lost without you.

Thank you Booktok! You are my people and I love you so much. Thanks for letting me be myself and accepting me into your amazing community.

And last but not least, I want to thank every single book blogger, influencer, reviewer, reader, and fan who has read my books and helped me share them with the world. I am eternally grateful. XOXO.

About the Author

M Violet is a dark romance author with a flair for the dramatic. She likes whiskey, rainy nights, and writing by the fire. When she's not creating scorching hot villains for you to fall in love with, you can find her eating chocolate and binge watching her favorite shows.

Facebook: Authormviolet
Instagram: Authormviolet
Tik Tok: Authormviolet

Made in the USA
Las Vegas, NV
20 January 2024